ai	Or
oa	Oa
or	Ai
ie	J
j	Ee
ee	Ie

Big, fat raindrops dripped and plopped.

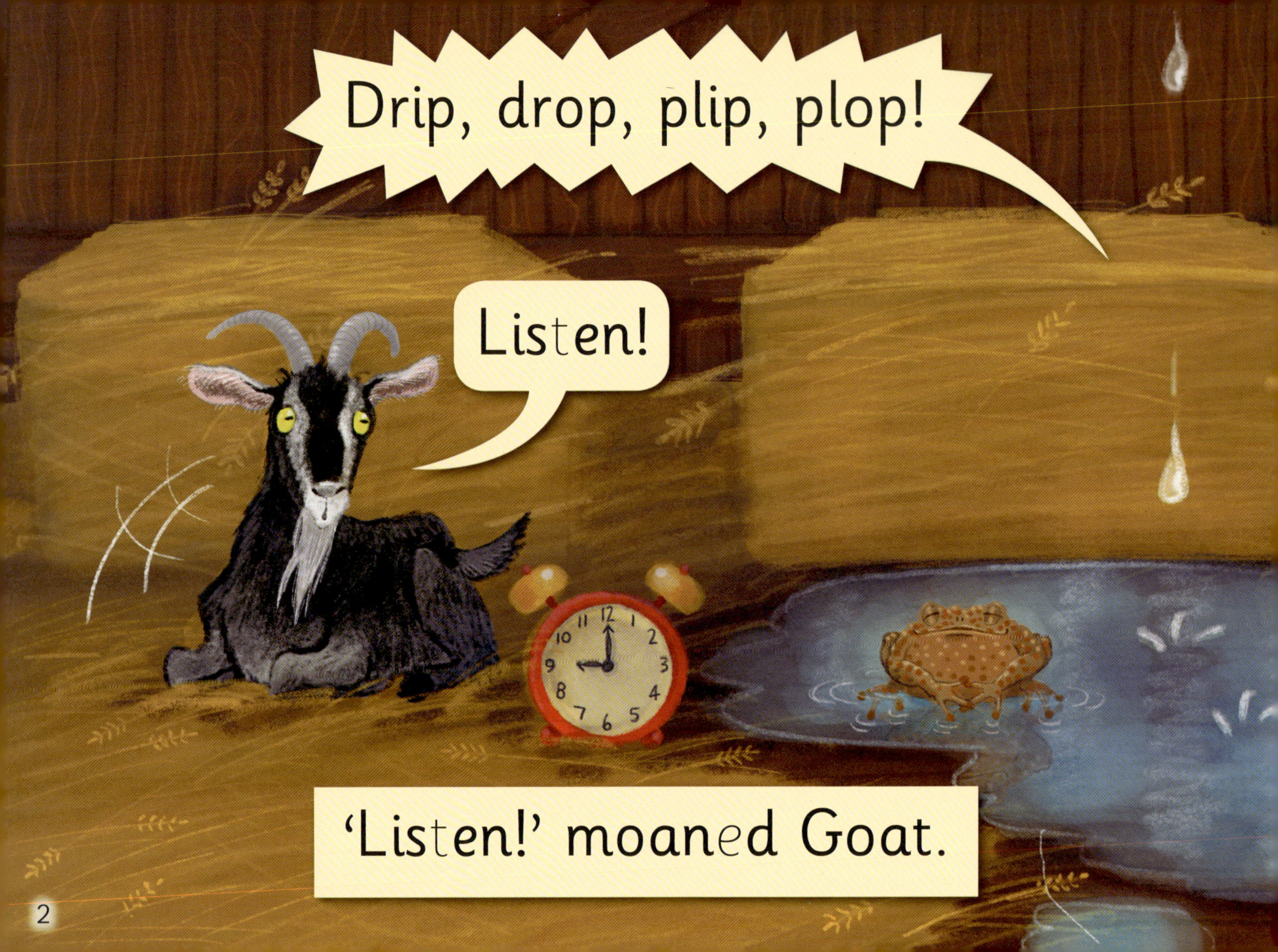
Drip, drop, plip, plop!
Listen!

'Listen!' moaned Goat.

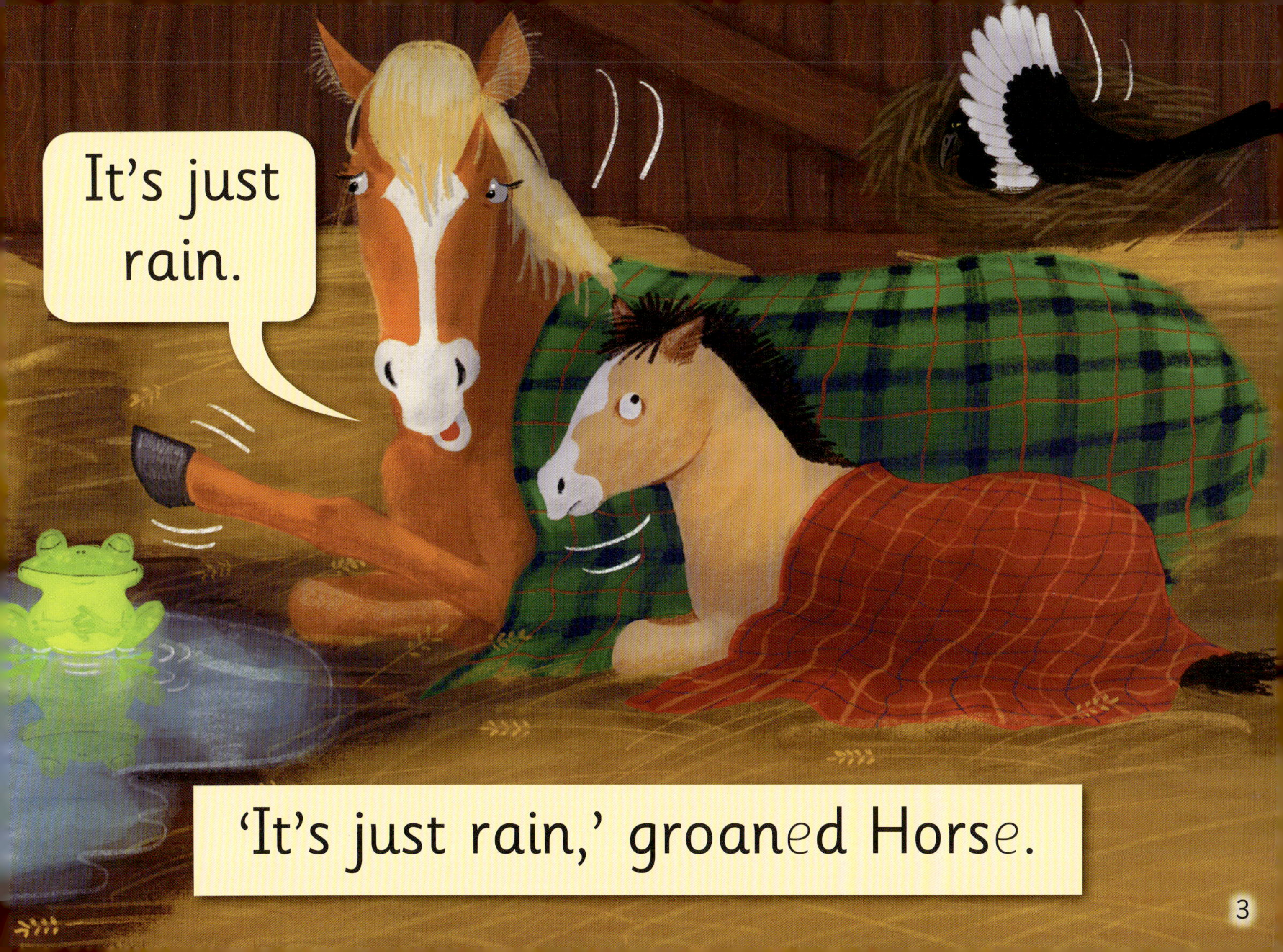
It's just rain.

'It's just rain,' groaned Horse.

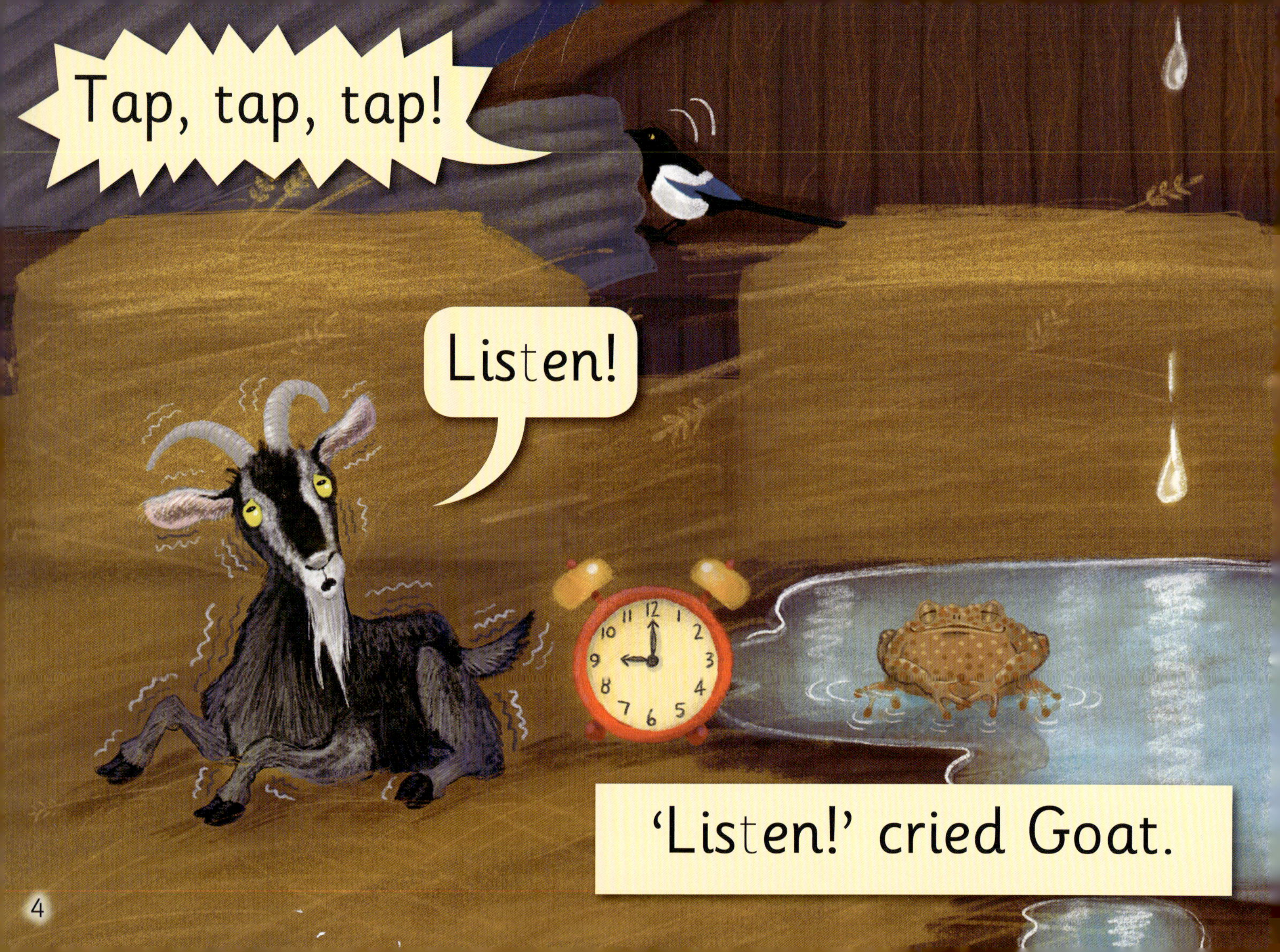
Tap, tap, tap!
Listen!

'Listen!' cried Goat.

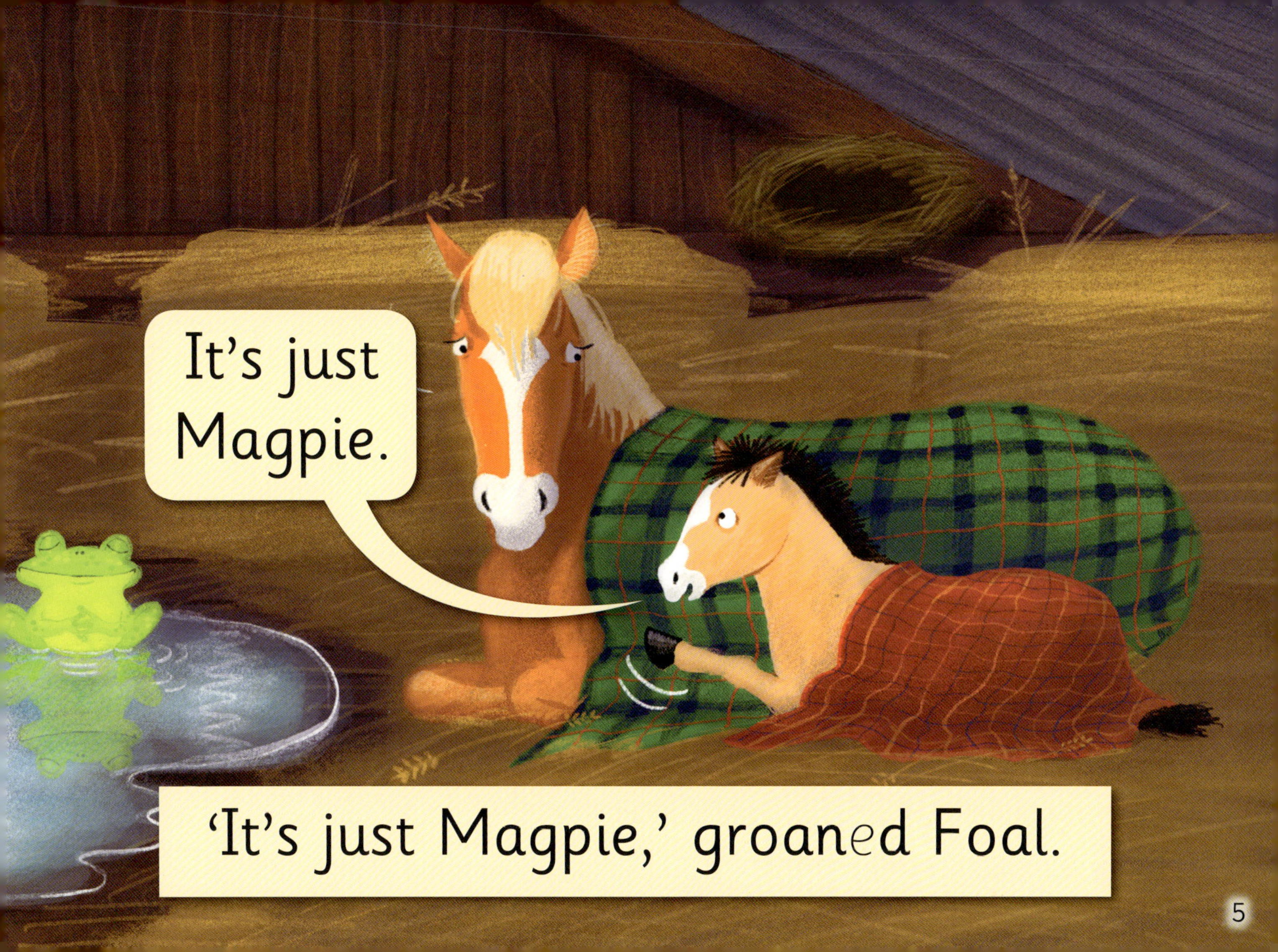
It's just Magpie.

'It's just Magpie,' groaned Foal.

Tick tock, tick tock!
Listen, listen!

'Listen, listen!' cried Goat again.

'It's just Toad's clock,' croaked Frog.

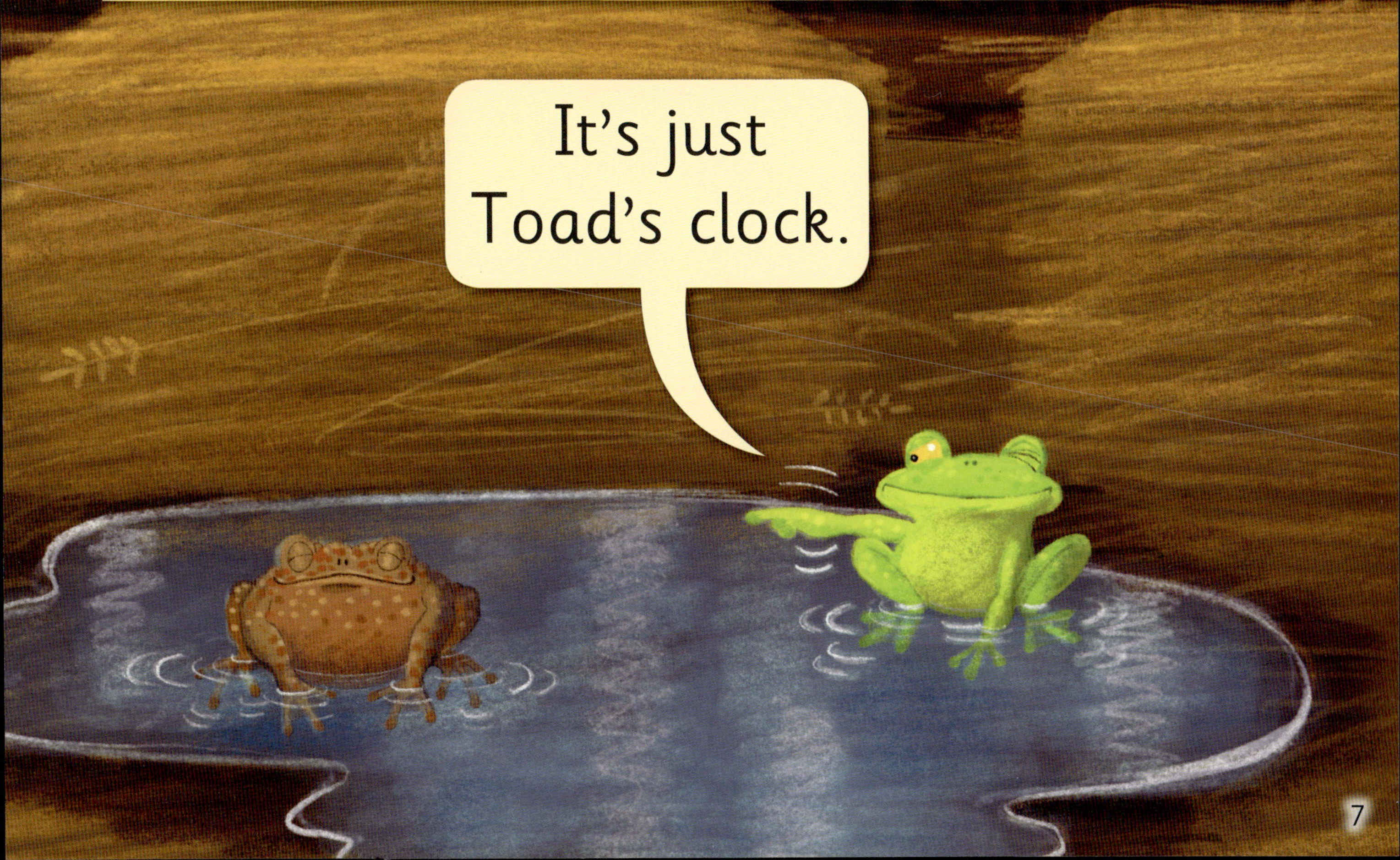
It's just Toad's clock.

At ten, Goat fell asleep.

Goat snored. Goat snored a lot.

Horse, Foal, Magpie, Toad and Frog jumped.

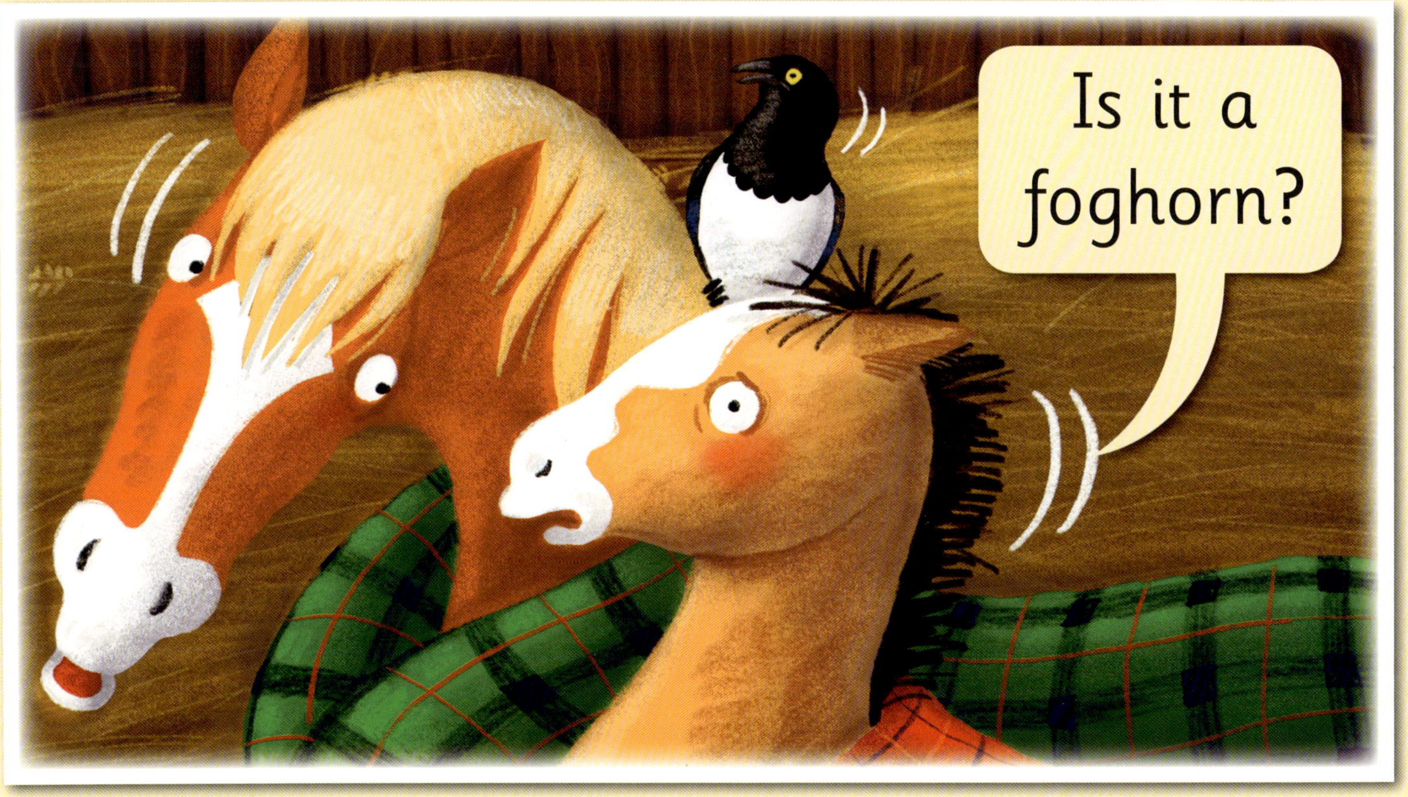
Is it a foghorn?

'Is it a foghorn?' cried Foal.

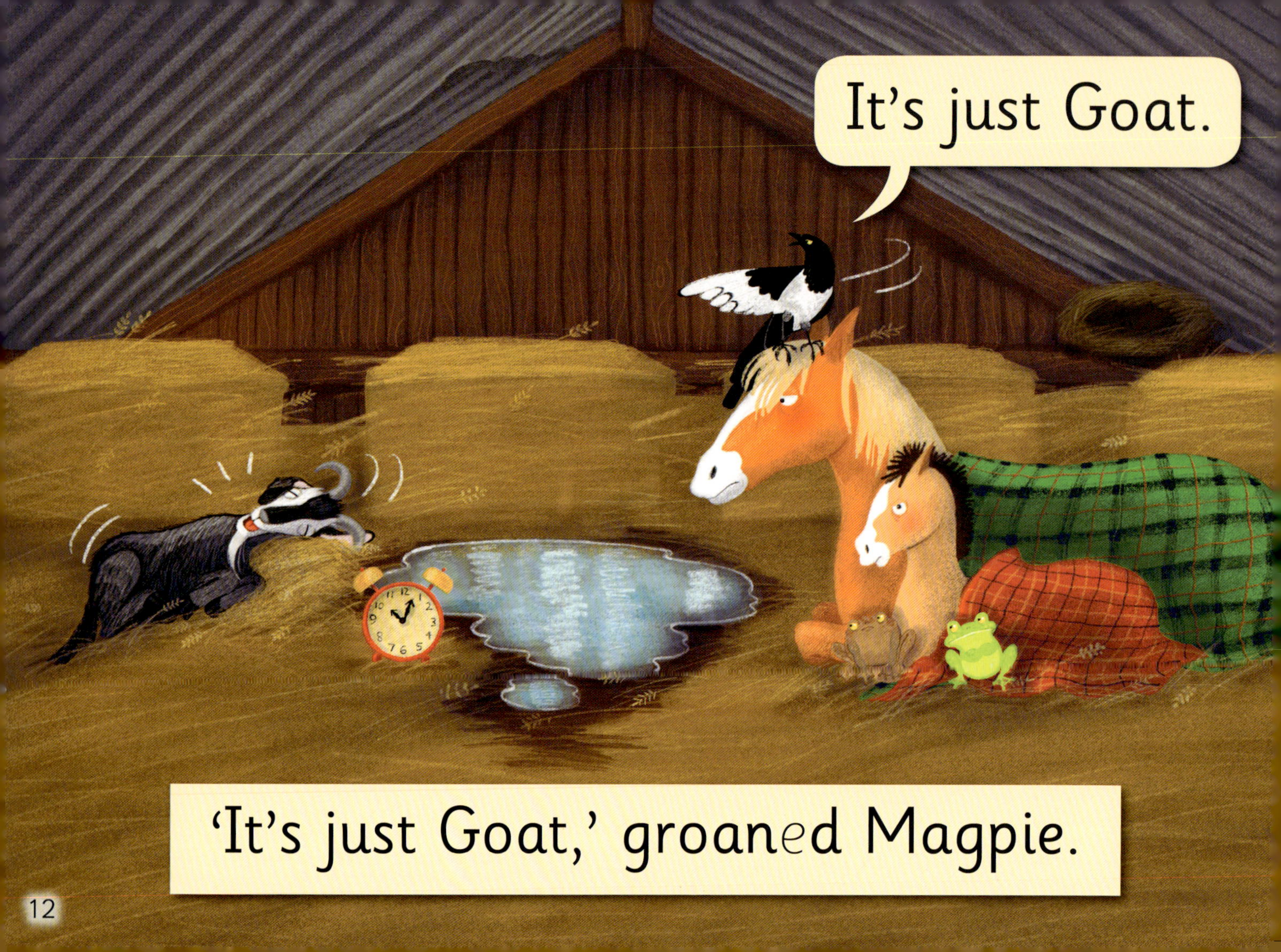
It's just Goat.

'It's just Goat,' groaned Magpie.